# The Ghost
## of Ichabod Paddack

Warren H. Bonton

# The Ghost
## of Ichabod Paddack

by Warren Hussey Bouton

Illustrated by Barbara Kauffmann Locke

Hither Creek Press
Short Hills, New Jersey

First Paperback Edition, 2002

The characters and events in this book are ficticious. Any similarity to real persons, living or dead, is coincidental and not intended by the author.

ISBN 0-9700555-2-8

Printed in the United States of America

*This book is dedicated to
loved ones past and present...*

# CHAPTER

# 1

"Hey, Sarah. Just because you're older doesn't mean you always get what you want!" Ben yelled as he pulled my stuff off the top bunk. Then, without another word, he jumped down from the bed and stood in the middle of the tiny bedroom we were going to share for the next seven days, glaring at me with his arms crossed in defiance.

"Knock it off, Ben!" I scowled. "Don't you think it's time you grew up a little and accepted that I am your superior in age, brains, and personality, and because of that should always get the top bunk! It's not just a place to sleep. It's a statement about the position I have in life as your OLDER sister. I belong in the top bunk and that means you get the place you deserve, the bottom!"

My little brother's face began to turn red. His eyes just about popped out of his head, and before I knew what was happening Ben grabbed the pillow off the bed and started to pound on me as he screamed, "I have rights too! Older doesn't mean better—it means that Mom and Dad saved the best for last!"

"Why, you little toad!" I shrieked as I grabbed the pillow from the top bunk and smacked Ben on the side of the head.

We kept beating each other with our pillows until finally our father yelled from the kitchen, "That's *eee-nough*! If you two are arguing about who's going to sleep on the top bunk, I'll settle it! You each get it for three nights apiece and we toss a coin to see who gets the extra night. Your Uncle Barney and I had the same fight when we were kids and that's the way it was solved, so I guess it'll work for you, too!"

Of all the trips that we had made to Nantucket this was the first time in many years that our whole family had been able to stay at my grandparents' cottage in Madaket. This year, instead of Ben and I traveling to the island on our own, Mom and Dad and even our golden retriever, Sadie, made the trip for a great family vacation on the beach.

The cottage was sacred to our family. My great-grandfather had built it 80 years ago on a quiet strip of sand on the western end of the island overlooking Madaket harbor. It was nothing fancy and it certainly wasn't big. The whole house was made up of a kitchen with an eating area, two bedrooms (one of which had the bunks we were fighting over), and a front room with a built-in couch, a single bed that doubled as a sofa, and a lot of old chairs. The bathroom was about the size of a postage stamp, and to take a shower you actually went outside to the shower stall, which was on the end of the house. There was no TV and no phone, but there was plenty of sun, sand, and ocean. The best part of it all was the wooden bench out in front. From there you could sit and watch the bay and the incredible summer sunsets. People traveled from all over the world to see a Madaket sunset and all we had to do was walk out the front door and there it was!

I was really excited that we were staying at the cottage this year. It wasn't just that the whole family was there—it also meant that Ben and I didn't have to stay at my grandparents' house. Now don't get me wrong. I love my grandparents and always have a great time with them. But the fact that their house on Main Street seemed to have more ghosts than people living in it made me more than a little nervous!

As far as I was concerned, this time we were going to be safe. There were going to be no ghosts, and no mysteries to be solved. It was just going to be a fun, relaxing vacation.

Little did I know that my brother Ben and I were about to begin one more spooky adventure!

# CHAPTER

# 2

As soon as we finished unpacking, Dad ducked his head into our room and asked, "Would somebody please put up the flag?" Putting up the American flag in the morning and taking it down every night was one of the traditions at the cottage. First thing every day, one of us would run out to the flagpole and raise the red, white, and blue. Then, right after sunset, down it would come. As far as Dad was concerned, if we were at the cottage and it was a nice day the flag needed to be flying, and even though it was late afternoon he had decided that it was time for the tradition to be renewed.

Ben and I both scrambled into the front room to find the flag sitting on a shelf right where it had always been. We scooped it up and ran out the front screen door, letting it slam behind us. Ben unlooped the rope from the lanyard on the flagpole. I secured the flag and then up it went, flapping in the breeze. "Get it all the way to the top, Ben, and then tie it tight." Of course, my little brother followed my excellent directions to the letter and we both

 stepped back to savor the sight.

With flag duties done, Ben began to run down the path to the beach. Scampering over the dunes with the

sand flying, he called over his shoulder, "Come on, Sarah, let's check out the beach!"

The tide was low and the beach was fantastic. The sun reflected on the blue, blue ocean and there was hardly a cloud in the sky. The sand was warm on our feet and there was just a little bit of a breeze that kept us cool as we walked. The beach slowly curved around to the north until it came to a point that looked like it must be at least a couple of miles away! You could tell where the high-tide line was because there was one long, narrow pile of dried brown and white eelgrass that had washed up during the last storm. I hated walking on the stuff, but Ben not only walked on it—he'd dig his hands into it, grab as much as he could hold, and then try to shove it in my face. And that's exactly what he was getting ready to do!

"Don't you dare, you little twerp!" I howled as Ben tossed a big wad of seaweed at me. I tried to duck, but instead of missing me it landed right on top of my head... a perfect hit! So there I stood with a wig of seaweed streaming down over my shoulders.

"Boy, Sarah," Ben giggled, "that's a real improvement! Now instead of just being a witch, you look like one too!"

I tore the gross, smelly weeds from my hair and started to chase my obnoxious little brother as he ran for his life over the sand dunes. By the time I finally tackled him, both of us were almost out of breath. "I ought to tie you up and throw you off the Madaket bridge for crab bait!" I huffed as Ben fell, curling up into a ball and laughing hysterically. He knew that once I'd caught him I wouldn't have the heart to even push his face in the sand. Ben may have been a monster, but after all, he was my baby brother.

As we sat in the sand enjoying the sun and sea, I finally noticed way out near the horizon what appeared to be a sandbar with something that looked like the skeleton of an old ship. There wasn't much left of it, just the keel, which is kind of like the ship's backbone, and a few ribs sticking up out of the sand. Pointing to it, I asked, "What do you think that is, Ben?"

"It's probably just an old wreck." But then he started making his voice sound creepy like he was telling a ghost story, and with wide eyes said, "Who knows, maybe it's a wreck that's haunted by spirits of its long-lost crew!"

It wouldn't be too long before we found out that his guess was almost right!

# CHAPTER

## 3

By the time we got back to the cottage, Dad had the grill going and hamburgers cooking. Mom had fresh corn from the local farm on the stove and was putting the final touches on a salad that Ben and I wouldn't touch with a 10-foot pole!

Burgers always taste so much better when they're cooked on the grill, and the corn was fantastic. It didn't take us very long at all to wolf down dinner. Mom and Dad went out to sit on the bench in front of the house while Ben and I struggled with clean-up duty.

"I'll wash and you dry. Grab a towel and let's get this over with!" I muttered as I splashed hot water into the kitchen sink.

"So what do you think is really out there?" Ben wondered.

"What are you talking about?"

"The wreck. Maybe it really *is* a ghost ship just waiting to lure unsuspecting boaters aboard and send each one off to a life of horror and doom!" Ben was enjoying himself just a little too much and was letting his imagination carry him away. There was a glint in his eyes and a sickening grin on his face as he spun around with the dish towel waving above his head.

"Stop it, Ben! You know that stuff spooks me out! I don't want to hear it!"

"Oh come on, Sarah, what's the matter?

A few ghosts every now and then never hurt anybody!"

Ben knew better than that! Just about every time we had come to Nantucket, the two of us had had more than enough experiences with spooks. The island seemed to be full of them. People had even written books about all the ghosts that were here, and a couple of times Ben and I had barely escaped with our lives because of the spirits we'd run into. The first was Captain Ichabod Paddack, who had almost swallowed us up forever in a nasty blue fog from an old sea chest in Grandma and Grandpa's attic. The next year it was a spirit named Cyrus who took us back in time and almost got us burned alive in the Great Fire of Nantucket. I'd had more than my fill of ghosts from the past.

"STOP! No more about ghosts!" I hissed. "Do you remember our friend Ichabod Paddack? Or how about Cyrus and the burning tree that almost turned you to toast? Do you really believe that 'a few ghosts every now and then never hurt anybody'? Get real! You can have my share if you want them!"

Ben became very quiet when I reminded him about Captain Paddack and Cyrus. In fact, he didn't say another word while we finished the dishes, and I didn't either. Both of us were lost in our own horrible memories of the spirits that we'd met on the island that felt to me like the ghost capital of the world.

# CHAPTER 4

When we had finished the dishes, Ben and I went outside to join Mom and Dad at the bench. The sun was almost ready to set, and the whole sky was an incredible blend of reds, yellows, oranges, and pinks.

"I love this place! It's so peaceful here," Mom said.

"It sure is—and red sky at night means sailor's delight!" Dad answered. "What's really amazing though is how fast the ocean can change. It's peaceful now, but believe me, when a storm comes up it can turn deadly out there very quickly. Sarah, when I was your age, my grandfather—that's your great-grandfather—drove my brother and me out here in his old blue Chevy pickup truck during Hurricane Esther. We stood inside the cottage and watched the surf break right over that low spot in the sand dunes just where the sun is about to set. It was incredible. Outside, the wind was howling and the surf was smashing over the beach, but in the house it was quiet and we felt so safe. The waves cut right through the dunes and broke the point off from the rest of the island. For years the part that was cut off was known as Esther Island until the sand finally filled in again."

"I wouldn't want to be out in a boat in a storm like that!" Ben piped in.

"That's for sure, a storm or fog!" Dad added. "It would be very easy for a boat to run into a sandbar out there."

"Dad, I spotted what looked like pieces from an old wreck quite a way out off the point. Did it run aground in a storm?" I wondered.

"No, that happened in a bad Madaket fog," Dad responded. "My grandfather once told me that back in the 1800s a whaling ship hit a sandbar out there. Once it ran aground, the seas started to get heavy and the ship began to break up. As far as I know, the keel and some of the ribs are still there, stuck in the sand. I think it was named the *Joseph Starbuck*. Come to think of it, there's an old sea chest up in Grandma and Grandpa's attic that came from that old wreck. Maybe you've seen it."

I couldn't believe what I was hearing. Ichabod Paddack had captained the *Joseph Starbuck*! The sea chest Dad was talking about had held Paddack's ghost and the horrible fog that had almost swallowed us alive. What was left of Paddack's ship was right there. I could see it off in the distance and I was terrified.

"Ben and Sarah, what's the matter? You've both turned as white as ghosts. You aren't coming down with something are you?" Mom worried.

"No...we're just fine," Ben and I answered almost in unison. "It's just that we did some research on the *Joseph Starbuck* a couple of summers ago when we were here visiting Grandma and Grandpa and we're surprised that the wreck is so...so...close."

The sun had set and as Mom and Dad headed inside, Dad called back, "It's time to take the flag down."

"We'll take care of it, Dad. We're just

going to hang out here for a little while," I answered.

Ben and I sat on the bench for a very long time without saying a word. We just stared out at the ocean where the wreck sat on its sandbar.

"What do you think, Sarah?" Ben questioned at last.

"I don't know!" I moaned with my head in my hands. "I just don't know, and I don't want to talk about it!"

We sat in terrified silence as the night grew darker and the stars became brighter. Ben finally took down the flag and headed inside.

A cool breeze began to blow in from the ocean and I decided to join the rest of the family. I had also decided that it was time to put the ghosts of summers past aside and enjoy my time in Nantucket. As I looked out at the wreck for one last time, I couldn't help but notice a strange blue glow out on the horizon right where the skeleton of the *Joseph Starbuck* was stuck on the sandbar. And then I heard someone calling my name. It wasn't Mom or Dad or even Ben. The voice was calling over the water.

> Sarah... Sarah... my dear young friend,.
> I've come for your precious help...
> I've come once again!

I ran into the cottage as fast as my legs could carry me, threw myself into my bunk, and pulled the covers over my head. I didn't care if my family thought I was crazy. I just couldn't stand the thought of being haunted by Captain Ichabod Paddack one more time.

# CHAPTER
# 5

By the time I woke up the next morning the sun was already pouring in around the edges of the window shade. It had taken me forever to fall asleep the night before, but once I had convinced myself that my imagination had just gotten the better of me I had finally drifted off.

"Hey Sarah," Ben yelled in from the kitchen. "Wake up—breakfast is ready. Dad and I are going to take Sadie for a run on the beach. Better hurry up if you want to come."

I really enjoyed taking Sadie to the beach. Golden retrievers love water, and Sadie got so excited when she had the chance to run and swim. It was one of her favorite things in the world to do.

Hauling myself out of bed, I threw on my bathing suit and a pair of shorts. After quickly downing some orange juice and a plate full of scrambled eggs that Mom had made, I was ready to go.

Ben and Dad had put the flag up and were waiting with Sadie at the bench as I hurried out the front door to join them.

"Come on, Sadie, it's time for some fun!" Dad said as he unhitched her collar, and in no time Sadie was running down the path at full speed. No sooner had she hit the beach than she was bounding into the water after a seagull that was floating about 15 feet from shore. The bird took off to avoid our rampaging dog, but Sadie just kept going. It looked as if she was willing to swim across the Atlantic Ocean if it meant catching that silly seagull.

When the bird was out of sight and Sadie realized that there was no catching it, she finally turned herself around and started back to shore. "Come on, Sadie, good girl!" we called as Ben, Dad, and I started walking up the beach. Before we knew it we could hear Sadie's paws pounding the sand behind us, and then she shot by like a rocket.

There was no stopping her. The more

seagulls she spotted, the harder she tried to catch them. One minute she was dog-paddling in the water and the next she was chasing a stray seagull over the sand dunes. In between, she kept running up to us to shake the water from her fur, soaking us to the skin!

The three of us had walked quite a way up the beach when suddenly we realized that we couldn't see Sadie anymore. She wasn't in the water and she wasn't ahead of us or behind us on the beach.

"Now where did she go?" Dad wondered aloud. "Sadie, Sadie!" he called at the top of his voice. When she didn't appear he sputtered, "It always happens. She gets so excited and is having so much fun that she just forgets to stay close. Tell you what—I'll stay here and keep an eye out for her. You kids run up that path and try to spot her on the other side of the dunes."

Ben and I scrambled up the path through the sand dunes until we came to what looked like a little fishing shack. The gray shingled walls were covered with weathered buoys. A pair of oars leaned up against the house next to a big pile of old scallop shells.

"This place has seen better days, if you ask me." I whispered to my little brother.

"I think it looks spooky," Ben answered with a shaky voice.

But the shack wasn't deserted. When we came around the corner of the house, there was an old woman standing straight as a board with her hands on her hips, staring down into the eyes of our golden retriever. Sadie was sitting at perfect attention meeting the old woman's gaze as if bewitched by some strange, ghostly spell.

# CHAPTER 6

"And who are you?" The woman asked as her stare slowly shifted from Sadie to us.

She was a weird sight. Tall and thin, she had a narrow face with a long nose. Her gray hair was pulled back tight into a bun, but a few pieces had gotten loose and looked like antenna coming out of the top of her head. What was strangest of all besides her cold dark eyes was the dress she was wearing—it looked like something out of the 1800s. It was long, running from her neck all the way to her ankles. It even had long sleeves which the woman had pushed partway up her arms.

"Wake up, children!" she shrieked. "I asked 'Who are you?' Are you going to just stand there and stare or are you going to tell me your names?"

"I'm Ben and this is my sister Sarah, and that's our dog Sadie." Ben stammered.

"Ben, Sarah, and Sadie are good strong names. Your parents could have done worse. But good names don't mean you're smart. You shouldn't let your dog run loose! There's no telling what kind of trouble she could get into."

"We were letting her run on the beach," I countered. "She loves to chase the seagulls and swim. But sometimes she gets excited and runs too far, too fast. That's all. We called for her but she either didn't hear us or she didn't listen."

"She listened to me just fine and I'm a stranger! You'd better work on making her mind you or someday she'll get lost for good. A beautiful creature like this is a real treasure. Don't take any chances. Now get out of here. Scoot! I've got work to do."

We took Sadie by the collar and started down the path toward the beach as the strange old woman watched with her hands on her hips and a serious look on her face. "My name's Hannah Hussey, by the way. You take care of that dog!"

Sadie hesitated, looking back as if she wanted to stay with old Hannah. "Come on, Sadie, let's find Dad," Ben whispered. That was all it took for Sadie to come with us without a struggle and her tail started to wag when she caught sight of Dad standing on the beach.

"It's about time," Dad called when he spotted us. "There's my girl. I thought we'd lost you for sure."

Sadie put her head down and nuzzled Dad's knees as he patted her head and rubbed her ears.

"Where did you find her?"

"You'll never believe this, but we found her with some old lady named Hannah," I said. "There's a fishing shack up there at the end of the path and Sadie was sitting there right at the woman's feet. It was strange, Dad."

It was strange all right. But at that moment I really didn't know just how strange!

# CHAPTER

We spent that afternoon at the beach. One of the things that was great about the cottage was that even though it overlooked a quiet little harbor, if we walked just a few minutes along a sandy road and over a path in the dunes we were at the surf.

The waves were pretty light, but we spent hours on our boogie boards and splashing in the water. Mom lathered us up with sunscreen so that we could spend just about all day in the sun without getting burned. Mom and Dad brought along their beach chairs and books. They were always perfectly happy to enjoy the sun and the view without getting wet. One thing they did like to do was stand on the very edge of where the waves broke and pick up rocks and shells that had been tumbled smooth by the water and the sand. Dad also loved to walk the beach. He was a beachcomber at heart, always stopping and bending down to pick up a new discovery. One time he managed to find 27 sand dollars in one walk.

"How about we hike up to the point, Ben?" I asked.

"I don't know. It's a long way."

"Come on, wimp!" I responded. "It's not as far as you think, and besides, we might be able to get a better view of that old whaling ship from up there."

"Are you sure you want to see it? After

all, I thought you were scared that the ghost of Ichabod Paddack was going to come and get you!" Ben teased.

"Shut up and let's walk!"

To be honest, I was scared of Captain Ichabod Paddack. But I had pretty much convinced myself that my imagination had gotten the best of me when I learned that his old ship was so close. Now I was just curious.

It was a long way to the point. By the time we got there we were both ready to sit down and take a break. It took us a minute or two, but we finally found a place in between the fishermen that had a good view of what was left of the *Joseph Starbuck.*

"I wonder what it was like to sail on a boat like that for three or four years at a time?" I wondered aloud.

"I don't know, but it must have been
pretty frustrating to get so close to home and
then wreck," Ben answered. "Captain Paddack
must not have been too bright!"

Suddenly a voice came from behind us. "You know about Paddack and the *Joseph Starbuck*, do you?"

We were startled to hear someone talking to us and just as surprised when we turned to see the gaunt form of Hannah standing within three feet of us.

"I wouldn't be talking about that ship or its captain if I were you," she said. "There's something evil about that wreck. I've seen strange things on these waters. Some nights there's been a blue glow coming from her, and a few folks say she's a ghost ship that still sails in the fog. Stay clear of her and don't be making up any stories about Paddack or you'll live to regret it!"

Ben and I looked back with wide eyes at the old wreck.

"Come on—do you really think it's haunted? I don't see how a grownup could..." But when I turned to face the old woman she was gone. She was nowhere to be seen. It was as if she'd never even been there.

"Where'd she go? She was just here a minute ago." I couldn't believe my eyes.

Then in a hushed voice Ben said what I was thinking: "This is getting spooky!"

# CHAPTER

Ben and I snuggled into our bunk beds that night ready for a good sleep. Between losing Sadie, the afternoon at the beach, our walk to the point, and our two meetings with Hannah Hussey, we were wiped out.

But even though I was exhausted, my mind kept running a mile a minute.

"Hey Ben, are you awake?" I whispered.

"If I said no, would you leave me alone?"

"What did you think of old Hannah?"

"I don't know," he said. "It doesn't really make any sense. One minute she's there and the next she's gone. She's creepy, if you ask me. Her eyes look right through you."

"I know what you mean. I wonder if she was already at the point when we got there or whether she followed us?"

"Maybe she got a ride in one of the fishermen's four-wheel drives!" Ben laughed.

"I don't think so. Nobody would give her a ride—not in that long dress she was wearing, and looking like an old witch."

"You don't think she's a witch, do you?" my little brother gasped.

"No, probably not. But I just can't stop thinking about what she said about Ichabod Paddack and that whaling ship. Could it really be haunted? I think we need to take a trip into town and see if Grandma and Grandpa have heard any stories about it."

"That would be cool," Ben yawned. "Maybe if we're lucky Grandma will be baking some of her chocolate chip cookies. Can I go to sleep now?"

"I suppose so. We'd both better get some sleep. Who knows what tomorrow will bring?"

My head swirled with images of Hannah, the *Joseph Starbuck*, blue fog, and strange sea captains. Maybe tomorrow I'd find some answers.

# CHAPTER
# 9

The ride to town on our bikes was long but fun! The bike path that runs beside Madaket Road weaves in and out of pine trees and moors. There are even a couple of places where it crosses over little bridges, and sometimes people are crabbing or watching the swans that call the pond their home. A lot of people use the path for everything from walking, jogging, roller-blading, and of course, cycling, so there's always something or somebody to see.

We had gotten a late start, and by the time we made it to Grandma and Grandpa's house in town it was almost lunchtime. When we pushed our bikes up the driveway we could tell that Grandpa was working on a project in his shop out back.

"Hello there, Sarah and Ben. What are you up to today?" Grandpa called as he stepped out of the shop to clean a paintbrush.

"We're just out for a bike ride and thought we'd stop by to say Hi," I answered. "We were also wondering if you know anything about that old wreck on the sandbar off the point. Dad says the ship's name was the *Joseph Starbuck*. Ben and I started to wonder about its captain and how it got wrecked."

"Don't know a thing about it. Your grandmother might, though. Her family has been around here longer than mine. You could probably find some information down at the

Whaling Museum or the Peter Foulger Museum, too. I'd bet you anything they would even have a logbook for it if you asked."

"I don't think we want the logbook," Ben responded. "That wouldn't have anything about the wreck. I kind of doubt they took the time to write in it while the boat was breaking up!"

"You've got a point there, Ben," Grandpa chuckled. "Well, maybe the library would have something. There's probably a bunch of books about all the old wrecks around the island. Might even be a book or two about the different whaling-ship captains. Seems like the kind of thing somebody would write about. Tell you what, how about you head into the house and see what Grandma has to say, and maybe she'll even fix you some lunch. Then you can head downtown and see what you can find at the library."

"Sounds like a plan to me," I said as my little brother and I headed for Grandma's kitchen.

# CHAPTER

# 10

As usual, Grandma stuffed us with food, giving us about twice as much lunch as we would normally eat. But we both knew that if we didn't clean our plates, we wouldn't get any of her fantastic homemade chocolate chip cookies, still warm from the oven.

"So, what do you have in mind for this afternoon?" Grandma asked. "Or did you ride all the way into town just for my cookies?"

"Well, not completely," I answered in between munches of cookie. "We spotted what's left of an old shipwreck out on a sandbar and we want to learn more about it. Ben and I thought we might go to the library and see what we could find. We also wondered if you might have heard a story or two."

Grandma replied, "I don't know much besides the fact that its name was the *Joseph Starbuck*—and we have that old sea chest from that ship up in the attic. Never could find a key that would open it. As light as it is, I'm sure it must be empty besides maybe a ghost or two! Come to think of it, I have heard an old tale that when the fog socks in real thick out in Madaket people have caught a glimpse of a ghost ship out near the *Starbuck*. They claim that they've even heard a voice calling out from it, but I just think their imagination has gotten away from them. It can get scary out there on the water in the fog."

Ben and I looked at each other with wide

eyes and I could feel the butterflies start to flutter in my stomach. "Ghost ship? Voices in the fog? I don't think I want to hear any more!"

"Oh don't be silly!" Grandma said with a smile. "It's all nonsense. People make up all kinds of stories just for the fun of it. If you really want to find out the truth about that old ship, why don't you go down to the library and see what you can find. And I tell you what—when you go, make sure you ask Louise Rounsville, that's Mrs. Rounsville to you, if she'll help you out. She's the head of research and has lived here for most of her life. She's not really an islander, but she has been on Nantucket for about 60 years. Louise knows just about everything there is to know about whaling and especially what's in that library. You tell her that I sent you down and let her know what you're looking for, and she'll not only save you a lot of time but she'll make sure you find exactly what you're looking for. By the time you leave that library you'll be experts on the *Joseph Starbuck*. You might even end up knowing more than you want to know."

Unfortunately for us, Grandma was right.

# CHAPTER
# 11

The library, which was officially known as the Nantucket Atheneum, is a great big white building with columns out in front. The huge main room echoed as we approached the desk. To be honest, Ben and I were more than a little nervous about asking for help, but when we saw the little old lady with a warm smile and "Louise Rounsville" on her nametag, we breathed a big sigh of relief.

"Now what can I help you with, children?" she asked.

"Mrs. Rounsville," I started, "our

grandmother told us that you could help us find some information about an old whaleship that went aground off Madaket. We think the name of the ship was the *Joseph Starbuck* and her captain was named..."

"The captain was Ichabod Paddack, if I remember correctly," Mrs. Rounsville responded. "Not a very pleasant man, if the stories about him are to be believed. In fact, he was known as one of the meanest captains ever to have sailed out of Nantucket. Tell me, why are you interested?"

"We spotted what was left of an old ship on a sandbar off Smith's Point in Madaket and...uh...we just wanted to learn more about it," Ben answered quickly.

"Well, I tell you what," Mrs. Rounsville said as she started to slide off her stool. "You two sit down at that table over there and I'll start to gather what I can find to help you out. I'm always happy when children want to learn more about the island and its history."

With that, Mrs. Rounsville started to shuffle around the library, stopping every once in a while to pull another book off a shelf. At last she came to our table with an armful.

As our new friend started laying the books before us, she told us about what she had found. "Now, let's see what we have here. According to this, Captain Paddack was not very well respected in the whaling industry on Nantucket. He was known as an angry and aggressive skipper who sometimes put his men at risk when at sea. On top of that, he had the reputation for bad judgment in the handling of his ship. It appears from what it says here that

another captain had been hired to take the *Joseph Starbuck* on what became her final voyage, but he became sick just before she was to sail. The owner had no choice but to hire the only whaleship captain left in Nantucket, and that was Paddack. That's about all this one says about him."

Mrs. Rounsville then put another open book in front of us. "This one says that after a very successful whaling trip of four years in the Pacific, the *Joseph Starbuck* was almost home when she was caught in a heavy fog just off Madaket. Instead of dropping anchor and waiting until it cleared, Paddack kept sailing and the ship landed hard on a sandbar. Shortly after they ran aground, the wind started to pick up and a fierce storm began to threaten the ship. The crew, afraid for their lives and fed up with Paddack's cruelty decided to take to the lifeboats, leaving him alone on the ship. It says here that it is assumed Paddack died when the ship broke apart. The final report about him said that he was last heard screaming at the top of his lungs that he would make them all pay someday and that he'd haunt the Madaket shores for all eternity until his ship was finally set free to sail again. He doesn't sound like the kind of person you'd want to invite to a party, does he children?" With that she noticed some other people looking for her help. "Oh, I'm sorry, children. I need to go and help these other folks. It was nice to meet you."

Ben and I couldn't say a word. All we could think of was the last line Mrs. Rounsville had read. Captain Paddack had threatened to haunt the Madaket shores forever. We sat there for a long time looking at the books until we suddenly heard a familiar voice from behind us. It was Hannah Hussey.

"I thought I told you children to forget about Paddack and his horrible ship!" she hissed. "That ship and that nasty man's ghost will be your doom. Leave him alone or the shores of Madaket won't be the only thing he haunts. He'll be haunting *you!*" Ben and I were both as white as sheets when we heard Hannah's words. We looked at each other with horror, and when we turned to look at Hannah again, she was gone.

It was a long bike ride back to the cottage that afternoon. We both kept our own thoughts and fears to ourselves. There was one thing we were both sure of—the ghost Ichabod Paddack wasn't finished haunting the waters off Madaket. But what really had us scared was that it looked as if Ichabod Paddack wasn't finished haunting *us*.

# CHAPTER
# 12

Dinner passed quickly. Mom and Dad couldn't understand why in the world we were being so quiet. They kept asking if we felt all right and whether something had happened on our trip to town. We knew we should tell them about Captain Paddack and the haunted ship. And we knew that we should say something about Hannah Hussey and how upset she had been at the library, but I guess we were both afraid that our parents would think we had gone nuts!

Dish detail came and went and neither

one of us complained or teased. I washed, Ben dried, and that was the end of it except for the horrible thoughts that raced through both of our heads.

Finally, Ben said, "Sarah, we need to talk. Let's head down to the beach."

To be honest, talking was the last thing I wanted to do, but at last I decided that maybe it would help. "Okay, if you really want to."

As we trudged by Mom and Dad, who were sitting on the front bench, I mumbled, "We're going for a walk and hopefully we'll be back!"

"Well, I sure hope so!" Mom answered with a chuckle.

We walked up the beach slowly not really lifting our eyes, just watching the sand squish through our toes as we ambled along. When we were far enough away so that our parents couldn't hear anything we might say, Ben at last piped in, "Sarah, we're letting our imaginations and that silly Hannah Hussey spook us out. This is stupid. So what if there is a wreck out there? Big deal! Captain Ichabod Paddack was a nasty old man! Who cares that some people claim to have seen a *ghost* ship in the fog? This is dumb! WE HAVEN'T SEEN A THING!"

"Ben, I know we haven't seen anything, but I *feel* something. I don't know what, but *something* is out there. And don't tell me that you don't believe in ghosts, because you and I have seen plenty when we've been on this island before."

Ben just shook his head. "I know, Sarah, but that's all over. You're just letting the ghosts of the past haunt your head now."

"But I heard Paddack again! The first night we were here. I heard him!"

"It was either your imagination, Sarah, or it was a dream. Get over it! I'm going to enjoy the rest of my vacation. I'm going to have fun. I'm going to play and take the skiff out for a row. I'm going to forget this silly ghost stuff, and you can either have fun too or sit in your room and sulk."

With that, Ben turned around and headed back to the cottage.

We didn't say another word to each other the rest of the night, not even when we crawled into our bunks. In my head, I knew Ben was right, but the butterflies in my stomach kept telling me that there was something spooky going on.

Just when I started to drift off to sleep, I

heard it again. That horrible scary voice filled my head.

> Sarah...Sarah...my dear young friend,
> I've come for your precious help...
> I've come once again!
> Don't be afraid. Don't you fret.
> The time to sail has not come yet.

I pulled the covers over my head and kept saying to myself, "It's only a dream. It's only a dream. Ben was right. It's your imagination, Sarah. There's nothing out there!" But there was something out there. Something Ben and I would see for ourselves the very next day.

# CHAPTER
## 13

The next day was beautiful. It was one of those incredible sparkling days that fills you with energy. I had pretty much convinced myself that I really was imagining all this ghost stuff. What I needed to do was just what Ben had said on the beach—forget about it and have some fun. Mom, Dad, Ben and I spent the morning crabbing over at Millie's bridge. Even though it was late in the season and Dad was sure the creek had been overfished, we still managed to catch four good-sized crabs and two whoppers. "Guess you'll manage to get a sandwich or two out of that bunch," Dad said to Mom as we walked back to the cottage. Mom was really the only one in our family who enjoyed eating crabs. Dad always called them bottom-feeders!

After lunch my parents decided to run into town to do some errands, but before they left Ben asked, "Dad, is it okay if Sarah and I take the skiff out for a row this afternoon?"

"It's all right with me, but I want you to stay close to shore. Don't go out very far, because before you know it you can get caught in a current and no matter how hard you row you'll never get back in without some help."

"Don't worry, Dad," I said. "I'll make sure he stays close to shore and behaves himself!"

"Good enough," Dad called back as he and Mom headed for the Jeep. "Come on, Sadie, want to go for a ride?" Sadie bounded for the car, jumped into the back, and off they all headed for town.

Ben got the oars from the garage while I found the life preservers. You never go out in a boat unless you have enough of the right kind of preservers for everybody aboard.

Down at the beach I pulled the anchor that held the skiff in place when the tide was high and we carefully got ourselves underway. At first, we headed right along the shore, but before I knew it Ben had the skiff pointed directly toward the old wreck.

"What do you think you're doing?" I screamed. "Dad told us to stay close to the beach."

"What Dad doesn't know won't hurt him! The only way you're ever going to believe that there aren't any ghosts is for you to see that that silly wreck is nothing more than an old pile of soggy wood."

"Ben, we don't have to go out there. I thought a lot about what you said last night and I can't believe I'm saying this, but you were right. I got spooked out. It was all in my imagination!" But no matter how hard I tried to convince him, Ben just kept right on rowing straight for the wreck of the *Joseph Starbuck.*

# CHAPTER

# 14

Ben seemed almost possessed. He just kept rowing and rowing. For the longest time I sat there with my head in my hands, staring at the bottom of the skiff.

"Uh-oh!" Ben groaned.

When I looked up I couldn't believe it— we were surrounded by a fog so thick I could hardly see my own hand in front of my face.

"Ben, when did this happen? Where did this fog come from?"

"I don't know. One minute we were in

the bright sunshine and the next everything was gray. I must have rowed into a fog bank and I just didn't see it coming. Look, I'll turn the boat around and before you know it we'll pop right out into the sunshine again."

Well, we didn't pop right out into the sunshine. Instead the fog just seemed to get thicker and thicker. Ben rowed as hard as he could until all of a sudden the skiff ran into something with an incredible thud.

"What in the world?" I screeched as both Ben and I were thrown off our seats.

"What is it?" Ben asked as he slowly picked himself up.

Neither one of us could believe our eyes. Somehow we had run into a huge sailing ship. It didn't seem to be moving, but there it was with three masts and all its sails up in the fog.

"This is weird," I whispered. "What's a ship like this doing here?"

"Who knows—but in this fog anything could happen," Ben answered. "Look—there's a rope ladder over there. Let's climb aboard and see who's around. I'd rather be on a big ship than a skiff as long as this pea soup is around."

"I don't know, Ben. I'm starting to get that spooky feeling again. This just isn't a good idea." But before I'd even finished, Ben was already climbing over the side of the ship.

A minute later he called down to me: "Sarah, get up here fast. You're not going to believe this!"

I scrambled up the ladder over onto the deck and found Ben standing perfectly still and staring at a big brass bell next to the ship's steering wheel. As I looked closer, I could see that the ship's name was etched into the brass. I suddenly felt a terrible chill run through my whole body. Ben and I were standing on the deck of a ghost ship. It was the *Joseph Starbuck.*

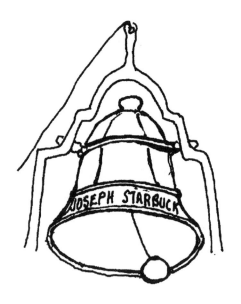

# CHAPTER
## 15

Before we had a chance to run for the ladder that would get us back to our skiff, a dreadful laugh came from behind us. As we turned we were horrified to discover a ghost materializing right before our eyes. It was Ichabod Paddack. When the captain's face became clearer with its piercing eyes and creepy smile, he said,

> Sarah and Ben, my dear young friends,
> How nice it is to see you again.
> You've come for a visit, to lend a hand.
> You're now my crew and I'll sail from
> this sand.

"We're not your crew. We're out of here!" Ben screamed as we started to run for the ladder and the safety of our little boat. But just before we went over the side Paddack laughed again and the rope holding the skiff untied all by itself. Then, while he hovered beside us, Paddack pretended to blow a kiss at our trusty craft. It was as if a great gale had sprung up out of nowhere and our boat drifted off out of sight in the fog.

> You ARE my crew, my precious young
>     friends.
> We will sail together 'til the world comes
>     to an end.
> The winds will blow, the waves will crash.
> The storm will come and free us at last.

And before we knew what was happening, the sky grew unbelievably dark. The wind began to blow, and the ocean around the

*Joseph Starbuck* started to boil and rock the old ghost ship.

Paddack let out a hideous laugh again.

The winds do blow, the waves run free,
You'll sail with Ichabod Paddack for all
    eternity!

As huge raindrops started to explode around us, Ben and I huddled beside the pilot house.

"We've got to get out of here, Ben," I shouted over the roar of the storm. This ship is going to break loose from the sandbar soon and we'll either end up as slaves to that crazy old ghost of a captain or land on the bottom of the ocean and haunt Madaket harbor ourselves. And if this thing sinks, you can bet anything that Paddack will be laughing all the way to the bottom."

Ben searched the deck with his eyes until suddenly he yelled, "Look, see those two little barrels over there? If we jump over the side with them we'll at least stay afloat in the heavy seas."

"You've got to be crazy," I screamed. "We'll drown for sure."

The ship rocked harder against the waves and the wind as Ben bellowed back, "Well I'd rather take my chances with a barrel in the storm than on a ghost ship that's already been wrecked once. Who are you sticking with, Paddack or me? He's not watching and I'm getting out of here *NOW!*"

As Ben leaped for the barrels the ship broke loose from the sandbar. Paddack, staring up at his full sails, let out a tremendous scream.

We're free, we're free!
Come my children, come sail with meeee.

That was it! Ben had made it to the barrels, picked one up, held it under his arm, and waved for me to hurry. I ran as hard as I could on the shifting deck, grabbed a barrel, and without another word or thought Ben and I dove over the side of the *Joseph Starbuck* into the black, churning sea.

# CHAPTER
# 16

As we hit the water, a huge wave washed over my head and I lost my grip on the barrel. I came up gasping for air. Flailing my arms desperately, I searched for something to help me survive. Just before another wave hit, Ben grabbed the back of my shirt and pulled me to his barrel.

"*SARAH*...hold on and kick!" he yelled.

Kicking for dear life to get away from the old whaleship, we heard Paddack's horrible screech when he realized we were no longer on board.

Nooo, I need my slaves, I need my crew.
I need your hands to sail the deep blue.
You ungrateful children, you failed to see
The honor it is to sail with me.
Foolish Sarah, foolish Ben,
I'll find you again and you'll never know
when!

The *Joseph Starbuck* then slipped into the fog and it was the last we saw of Captain Ichabod Paddack.

"He's gone." I shouted to Ben. "Now let's get out of here too. Kick!"

We kicked and paddled as best we could while hanging onto the barrel. A bunch of waves washed over us, but slowly and surely the storm started to die down and the waves began to ease. We were both exhausted and waterlogged.

"I don't know how much longer I can hang on, Ben."

"You have to, Sarah. Don't give up. Just hold on and we'll make it to shore before you know it. Hey, look!" My little brother shouted. "There's the skiff. It's still floating. Come on!"

With new life and energy, we kicked our hearts out and at last reached the skiff. It had about three inches of water sloshing around in it, but neither one of us was about to complain. Ben pulled himself over the side and then I carefully struggled out of the water and into our faithful little boat. The oars were gone, but I couldn't have been happier if I was sailing on the most beautiful cruise ship in the world.

"It may not be much," I grinned, "but it's just perfect for me!"

If only that had been the end of our little trip.

# CHAPTER
# 17

Paddling with our hands, we seemed to be making really good progress. The clouds were still gray and the wind was still a little gusty but at least the fog had cleared off and we knew exactly where we were.

"I can see the flagpole in front of the cottage," I called out with excitement.

"Sarah, I know I shouldn't complain," Ben mumbled, "but I think we're in trouble again."

"What do you mean? The storm is over. We're almost back to the shore. The cottage is there. The point is there, and Tuckernuck..."

Before I could finish, my little brother muttered with panic in his voice, "That's just what I mean. I think we're caught in the current that runs between the point and Tuckernuck. We're drifting toward the opening."

"So what's the big deal?" I asked.

"The big deal is if we don't get tipped over and drown in the white water of the opening where the currents run into each other, there's nothing between us and Spain except 3000 miles of ocean! And no offense, but I don't want to cross the Atlantic with you in a 10-foot skiff!"

"Well, if that's the way you feel about it, let's *PADDLE!*"

Both of us reached over the side and paddled as hard as we could with our arms, but no matter how much we tried, the current kept pulling us closer and closer to the opening. The water started getting really choppy again and tossed our tiny boat from one wave to another as we moved faster and faster. At one point the skiff almost flipped right over as waves hit us from both sides. We were in big trouble. I was positive we were lost for sure.

"Look, there's Hannah!"

The point was completely deserted. The fishermen had all run for town when the storm had rolled in, but there was Hannah, standing on the edge of the point with waves thrashing around her ankles. She stood there gauging the way the current was pulling us. We really weren't very far from shore, but the raging white water wasn't going to give us up to the beach. Suddenly, we realized that Hannah had a rope in her hands.

"Be ready, children. You'll have just one chance!" she yelled.

With that, she threw the rope as hard as she could and it landed right across the middle of the skiff. We both scrambled to get it and bumped our heads as we met in the middle, but we held on for dear life. Hannah slowly strained and pulled until the skiff was hauled free of the

white water and we could jump from the boat. Ben and I dragged our little rowboat as far up on the beach as we could and then collapsed.

"Are you all right, my children?" Hannah asked. "I *told* you to stay away from that wreck and that awful Captain Ichabod Paddack. It almost cost you your lives, and then your parents and dear Sadie would have been very sad. Listen to this old lady the next time and you'll save yourself a lot of trouble."

Having spoken her mind, Hannah turned and started walking back toward her shack. As Ben and I watched her go we couldn't believe our eyes when she slowly faded and disappeared into thin air. Shaking our heads in wonder, we looked at each other and rolled our eyes. As we collapsed into the sand we both gasped, "Not her, too!"

# CHAPTER
# 18

That night Grandma and Grandpa came out to Madaket for dinner. Somehow we had managed to put together a good enough story to keep ourselves out of trouble with Mom and Dad. Ben and I had agreed that we'd keep certain pieces of our horror story to ourselves—especially the parts about the captain and Hannah. We all went outside to the bench after dinner and Dad was the first to look out toward the sandbar and notice that what had been left of the *Joseph Starbuck* was no longer there.

"That must have been quite a storm this

afternoon. After all these years it looks like that old whaleship is finally gone. Maybe it's sailing the deep blue sea again," Dad chuckled.

Grandma piped back, "Either that or it's floating in the fog like some of the ghost stories claim."

My brother and I just looked at each other and didn't say a word.

After a little while I finally gathered the courage to ask, "Grandma, do you know an old woman out here in Madaket named Hannah?"

"Now where did you hear about Hannah Hussey? Hannah lived in Madaket just about all her life." Grandma replied. "She walked the beaches with her dogs. Kept an eye on the sea and always seemed to know what was going on out there. There are all kinds of stories about her helping troubled boaters, especially folks trapped in the current over at the opening between the point and Tuckernuck. But she died years ago. Hannah was quite a character. I wouldn't be surprised, though, if her ghost still walks the shoreline in search of people in trouble."

Ben and I looked at each other and said aloud exactly what we were both thinking: "It wouldn't surprise us either, Grandma. Not one bit!"

Look for more spooky tales by
Warren Hussey Bouton

# Sea Chest
## in the Attic

and

# The Ghost
## on Main Street

For information about
Hither Creek Press
or to contact the author
send your email to:
Hithercreekpress@aol.com